Mole's Cousin
by Rosemary Anne Sisson

Book version by Nicholas Jones

Illustrations from the Cosgrove Hall production
Directed by Jackie Cockle

Thames Methuen

First published in Great Britain 1984
by Methuen Children's Books Ltd
11 New Fetter Lane, London EC4P 4EE
in association with Thames Television International Ltd
149 Tottenham Court Road, London W1P 9LL

Copyright © 1984 by Cosgrove Hall Productions Ltd

Book version © 1984 by Thames Television International Ltd
and Methuen Children's Books Ltd

Printed in Great Britain

ISBN 0 423 01160 X

Mole's Cousin

Mole End, one has to admit, was not the most
fashionable of residences: after all, Mole was not
rich, like Toad, or artistic, like Rat. He was not of
ancient lineage, like Badger. But Mole had built
Mole End himself, to suit his own modest tastes,
and he was fond of it, with its Gothic windows,
its bell-chain and its lamp. Anyone who came to
visit Mole always felt welcome, and people *did*
come: Rat, if he could be enticed away from his
beloved River; Toad, to play skittles, and even
Badger would share a glass of home-brewed ale.

But Mole never expected visitors from the bigger world outside – at least, not until a letter arrived one morning. 'O my!' he exclaimed, as he read it on his doorstep. 'I must tell Ratty!'

As he neared the riverside house, it became obvious that Ratty was not alone. Toad's voice rang clear in the bright morning air, and Toad was at his most bumptious:

'One has one's duty,
dear old Rat,
as a leader of society.
Wealth has its duties,
as well as its privileges,'
he was saying.
'One endeavours to
elevate the tone . . .'

Ratty could stand this no more, and endeavoured
to bring Toad down to earth. 'Care for a cup of
tea, Toad?'

Such tactics could not stop Toad – he merely
incorporated the suggestion in his grandiose
thoughts: 'Tea? Why not, dear Rat? Soon it will
be caviare, champagne. But now . . .'

'Ratty!' Mole called as he neared the front door.
This provided the diversion the Rat needed.
'There's Mole,' he remarked to Toad.

'O, Mole. An excellent fellow, Mole,' Toad
replied magnanimously, although he then rather

spoiled the effect by adding, 'in his way.'

Mole could scarcely contain his excitement as Ratty opened the door to him. 'Hullo, Ratty! Toad, I'm glad you're here. Such news, Ratty!'

'Come in, old fellow,' Ratty welcomed his friend warmly. 'Care for a cup of tea?'

'O, yes please! I didn't have any breakfast. You see, I got this letter –'

Mention of letters reminded Toad of what he had been talking about. 'Ah, Mole! Just in time to hear my news.'

'I have some news too, Toady. You see, I had this letter . . .'

'Ah, yes. Don't get many of those, Mole, I dare say? Now *my* correspondence extends throughout the crowned heads of Europe . . .'

The other two animals were determined not to give Toad the attention he sought. 'Here's your tea, Mole,' said Rat.

'Thank you Ratty. Yes, I've had a letter from my cousin, and, O, Ratty, he's coming to stay with me!'

'I say, Mole, that'll be jolly for you,' said the Rat, genuinely pleased at his friend's excitement. Toad was less impressed:

'Yes, yes, very interesting,' he said, impatiently, 'but Mole, you haven't heard *my* news yet . . .'

'Sugar, Toad?'

'What? O . . . yes.'

The diversion just gave Rat time to enquire, 'What sort of a chap is your cousin, Mole?'

'Well, I've never actually met him, but I dare say he likes the same sort of things as I do. Ratty, I thought you could perhaps show my cousin the River. We might even have a picnic. And I'm sure he'd like to visit Toad Hall . . .'

Toad seized this opening, gulped down his tea, and began:

'Dear Mole, any relative of yours, however humble, must always be welcome, but just now a Rather Important Social Event is about to occur. I am giving a Literary Soirée, and have just heard that the distinguished poet Auberon Mole has promised to attend.'

'O, yes,' said Mole, matter-of-factly. 'That's my cousin.'

Toad's mouth dropped. Impossible!

Even Ratty looked startled. 'Auberon Mole is your cousin, Moley?'

'No, no, Ratty, of course not!' Toad burst out. 'Auberon Mole is a famous literary figure. Mole's cousin is someone *quite* different.'

Mole, simple fellow that he was, did not take offence at Toad's attitude, but replied calmly:

'I daresay he is, Toady, but his name *is* Auberon.'

Despite this evidence, even Rat still doubted Mole a little, and he enquired, 'I say, Mole, are you sure?'

In reply, Mole pointed to the letter. Rat perused it, and said simply, 'Quite right. So it is.' He looked sternly at Toad, who insisted,

'But he is a famous literary figure! I was quite astonished when he agreed to come to our little soirée. Naturally, I suggested that he should stay at Toad Hall. He can't possibly stay at *Mole End*!'

Mole looked despondent. 'O.'

'Rot, Toad!' Rat retorted. 'Of course he can!'

Mole smiled, relieved.

Ratty continued, 'Mole End is a very jolly little place. It just needs furbishing up a trifle. No difficulty with that, eh, Moley?' At this, Mole looked a little uneasy, but he nodded.

And so, a day or two later, the two friends came to give Mole a hand. There was plenty to do, as Toad and Rat saw the task. For instance, the garden roller needed to be hidden. A pot of chrysanthemums might do the trick, Ratty reckoned:

'That's right Toad – put it down there,' he directed.

'But I use the garden roller every day,' Mole objected. 'Rabbits *will* come and make footprints, and I like to keep the place tidy.'

'But you don't want to look as if you do it yourself, Mole,' Toad replied. 'Why not hire a weasel for an hour or so every day to lean on it? That's what my gardeners do at Toad Hall.'

Rat kept finding things which he considered unfitting for the important guest. 'And we really ought to hide the skittles.'

'O yes,' Toad agreed, conveniently forgetting how much he had enjoyed his games on Mole's front path. 'Not the thing at all for a *gentleman's* house!'

'We might borrow one of Badger's cricket bats – prop it up outside the front door,' continued Rat.

*   *   *

When they went to collect the bat, Badger had a few other suggestions. 'Nothing like a Latin quotation or two, my young friend,' he suggested. 'When occasion arises, just take one of these books negligently out of your bookshelves . . .'

When they had staggered back to Mole End with Badger's books, Rat transferred his attention to the surroundings. 'We really ought to do something about this furniture,' he remarked. So, in due course, some of Toad's choicest pieces arrived.

Placid though he was, Mole was beginning to feel threatened, and he plucked up the courage to object. 'I'm not sure that . . . er . . . quite fits with the rest of my furniture,' he said, cautiously.

It didn't occur to Toad *why* Mole might have doubts. 'I should hope not, Mole,' he replied, devastatingly. 'That's Chippendale, that is!'

The Rat, meantime, placed the candelabra on the table. 'You'll dine at home, Mole, the first evening, I dare say?'

The prospect horrified Mole. 'Dine?' he quavered.

Toad, still quite insensitive to Mole's feelings, suspected it was the food that was the problem. 'Don't worry, Mole,' he said. 'I'll send the food round – caviare, chateaubriand, champagne . . .'

'Yes, but . . .' Mole tried to stem the flow of suggestions.

'And, of course, you'll change for dinner,' Rat said, in a tone which implied that there could be no doubt about it. Even he had not realised Mole's true concern, and continued, when he received no immediate reply,

'Ah, no dinner jacket, I dare say. Toad?'

'Certainly, my dear fellow. Only too happy to oblige.'

The previous Michaelmas, Toad had written a little song for his entertainment at Toad Hall. 'You've Got to have Style,' it was called, and it exactly summed up what the three friends were trying to say to Mole. Toad tentatively tried the first line – and the others joined in:

You've got to have a little bit of style.
If you leave it all to us,
You'll be really quite beguiling.
Casually quote a Greek or Latin phrase,
Or something from the tragic plays of Shakespeare.
You've got to have a little bit of style.

You've got to have a little bit of style.
That's the thing that always
Knocks them in the aisles.
Just be scintillating, debonair and chic.
And I can give you hints on after dinner speaking
Then you'll have a little bit of style.

You've got to have a little bit of style.
If one is not too gifted,
It's terribly worthwhile
To know about antiques and *objets d'art*,
And maybe drop in little gems like Eton and Haa-row:
Show you've got a little bit of style!

You've got to have a little bit of style!
It'll help you through those really rather
Terribly vile occasions
Where everyone's acting affable and suave.
And polishing off the champers and the Graves by the magnum.
Then you need a little bit of style.

You've got to have a little bit of style!
High society people
Stand out by a mile
'Cos they're fashionable, elegant and astute,
Though a slightly pinching waist is causing acute discomfort.
You've *got* to have a little bit of style.

An hour later, Mole was looking at a reflection of himself which he scarcely recognised. His three friends were still making encouraging remarks, although Rat implied that it could have fitted better. 'Er . . . splendid, Moley,' he said.

'If only we had time to get it to my tailor,' Toad remarked.

Mole glanced
at himself
once again
in the mirror,
and he could
finally contain
himself no longer.
'No!' he said, defiantly.

Rat, Toad and Badger looked at each other,
astonished. 'No?' they echoed.

'No!' Mole repeated. 'If he won't take me as I
am, he can . . .' Losing his temper was so foreign
to Mole's nature that he was stuck for words, and
he had to finish, a little lamely, 'he can . . . go
away!'

It was therefore in his neat but homely clothes

that Mole welcomed an impeccably dressed cousin on the following day.

'So this is Mole End!' Auberon said, as he crossed the threshold. After all his friends had tried to do, Mole assumed Auberon would be critical of his humble surroundings, so his tone was defiant when he replied, 'Yes, it is!'

His suspicions were confirmed when Auberon asked, 'Should I dress for dinner?' so he said: 'No. And I don't usually have dinner. Just high tea.'

'Ah!' said Auberon, non-commitally.

Mole had a touch of desperation in his voice as he continued: 'I thought we might have muffins and poached eggs,' so he was astonished when Auberon replied, 'Just what I fancy!'

'Really?' Mole perked up.

'And – just the two of us?'

Even now unsure of his cousin's true wishes, Mole replied tentatively, 'Er . . . yes.'

His fears were finally dispelled when Auberon replied, 'Splendid. If you only knew how tired I am of High Society and Literary Figures, and all that stuff!'

As they sat, feet up, beside the fire later that evening, Auberon continued:

'I don't mean to do anything while I'm here except enjoy a little simple comfort and some family gossip.'

'Did you know about Uncle Ethelbert . . . ?'

The next morning, Auberon and Mole played skittles. 'I've *always* wanted to play skittles,' enthused the delighted Auberon, and, 'Most refreshing – what a treat!' when Mole served some home-brewed beer. 'We don't really have to go to that Literary Soirée tomorrow, do we?' he asked.

Mole, warmed though he was by this turn in events, felt loyal to his friend. 'Toad will be so disappointed if you don't. I think you ought to go.'

'O, very well. Just to please you!'

So the next evening, Toad, in his grandest evening dress, came to collect his honoured guest, and they returned to Toad Hall in

Auberon's chauffeur-driven Rolls – even if it caused Toad some discomfort to note that the chauffeur was another *toad*!

Arrived at the Hall, Toad received his come-
uppance in full measure.

'What a charming little
place you have here,'
Auberon remarked.
'It quite reminds me
of the Summer House
at Little Bending,
the Duke of Pilling's
place.'
'Summer house?'
spluttered the
outraged Toad,
but Auberon continued,
including Mole in
an expansive gesture,
'You know my cousin, of course. When I
received your – very obliging – invitation, I was
going to refuse . . . Such a press of engagements.
So fatiguing. But then I realised it would give me
the opportunity to visit Mole End, and to get to
know my cousin. I remember that my father

always used to say that he was the best of the lot of us.'

Toad couldn't believe his ears. '*Mole*?' But Ratty responded, 'Quite right. So he is,' and Badger said, with his usual dignity, 'An honour and a privilege, Sir, to welcome you here. Not least because you are related to our friend.' Toad realised which way the wind was blowing. 'What? O. Yes. Quite so, Rat. Absolutely, Badger. You took the very words out of my mouth . . .'

The Soirée was a great success, and Auberon was captivated by his cousin's hospitality. When the time came to leave, Auberon was fulsome in his thanks:

'Dear Cousin. I can't thank you enough. I feel a different Mole. I hope I may come back again one day.'

'Any time, of course,' said the delighted Mole.

'Perhaps, next time, Ratty would take me on the River?'

'I'm sure he would! Goodbye, Cousin Auberon!'

A few days later, the front-door bell jangled. It was Toad. 'Hullo, Mole!' he beamed. 'Just wondered if you might care for a little game of skittles?'